Little Colt's
PALM
SUNDAY

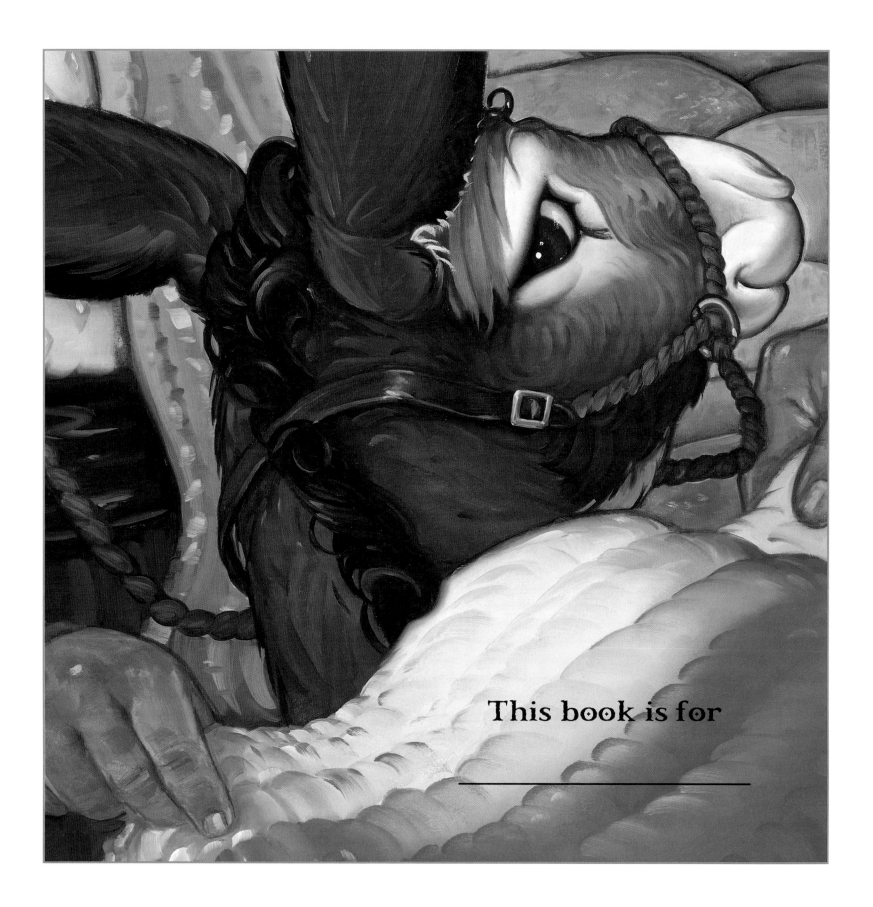

This book is for

_____

Little Colt's
PALM SUNDAY

Written by Michelle Medlock Adams

Illustrated by Wayne Parmenter

ideals children's books.
Nashville, Tennessee

ISBN 0-8249-5503-X

Published by Ideals Children's Books
An imprint of Ideals Publications
A division of Guideposts
535 Metroplex Drive, Suite 250
Nashville, Tennessee 37211
www.idealsbooks.com

Color separations by Precision Color Graphics, Franklin, Wisconsin]

Printed and bound in Italy by LEGO

ALSO BY MICHELLE MEDLOCK ADAMS

Conversations on the Ark
The Sparrow's Easter Song
My Funny Valentine

10 9 8 7 6 5 4 3 2 1

Designed by Eve DeGrie

Library of Congress Cataloging-in-Publication Data

Adams, Michelle Medlock.
    Little Colt's Palm Sunday / written by Michelle Medlock Adams ;
illustrated by Wayne Parmenter.
        p. cm.
    Summary: A young donkey asks his mother to retell how his great-great-
grandfather once carried the mother of Jesus while she was with child, then
learns for himself how marvelous it feels to do something for God.

    ISBN 0-8249-5503-X (alk. paper)
    [1. Donkeys–Fiction. 2. Jesus Christ–Entry into Jerusalem–Fiction. 3. Palm
Sunday–Fiction. 4. Stories in rhyme.]   I. Parmenter, Wayne, ill. II. Title.

PZ8.3.A10036Li 2004
[E]–dc22

2004015408

For Mindy Leigh, my sweet niece–
You are so precious to me!
Love you! "Aunt Missy"–M.A.

For my wife, Anna–
Without her love and support this book
would not be possible–W.P.

Go to the village ahead of you, and as you enter it, you will find a colt tied there, which no one has ever ridden. Untie it and bring it here. If anyone asks you, 'Why are you untying it?' tell him, 'The Lord needs it.'"

Those who were sent ahead went and found it just as he had told them.

As they were untying the colt, its owners asked them, "Why are you untying the colt?"

They replied, "The Lord needs it."

They brought it to Jesus, threw their cloaks on the colt and put Jesus on it.

As he went along, people spread their cloaks on the road.
—Luke 19:30–36

The young colt snuggled in the hay.
He fidgeted about.
"Please go to sleep," his mama said,
And then she kissed his snout.

"But, Mama," whispered Little Colt.
"I'm just not sleepy now."
"Shh, shh, be quiet," Mama said.
"You'll wake up Mrs. Cow."

"Will you tell me a story, Mom?
I promise to be still."
"Okay," the mama donkey said.
"For you, my son, I will.

"While donkeys live quite humble lives,
Sometimes we do great things.
In fact, your great-great-grandfather
Once helped the King of Kings."

"He did! But how?" asked Little Colt.
His eyes became quite wide.
"He carried Mary," Mama said,
"And Jesus was inside."

"Inside?" asked Colt. "What do you mean?"
The mama donkey smiled.
"Let me explain," she softly spoke.
"See, Mary was with child.

"Your great-great-grandpa carried them.
With every step, he knew
That someday Mary's baby boy
Would have great things to do.

"And he was absolutely right,"
The mother donkey said.
"That Jesus does great miracles.
He's raised men from the dead!"

"Oh, Mama!" whispered Little Colt.

"I want to meet this man!"

Then Mother Donkey nuzzled him.

"Maybe, someday you can.

"But now you need to go to sleep.

You promised, little one."

"Okay, Mama," said Little Colt.

"But sleeping is no fun!"

The morning sun awakened them.
It gently warmed the hay.
"Come on, Son," Mama Donkey urged.
"We've got to work today."

Then suddenly, their owner came
And led them into town.
He tied them up and softly spoke:
"I won't be long. Don't frown."

"I've never been to town," said Colt.
"Why do you think we're here?"
"I'm not sure," Mama Donkey said.
But soon, it would be clear.

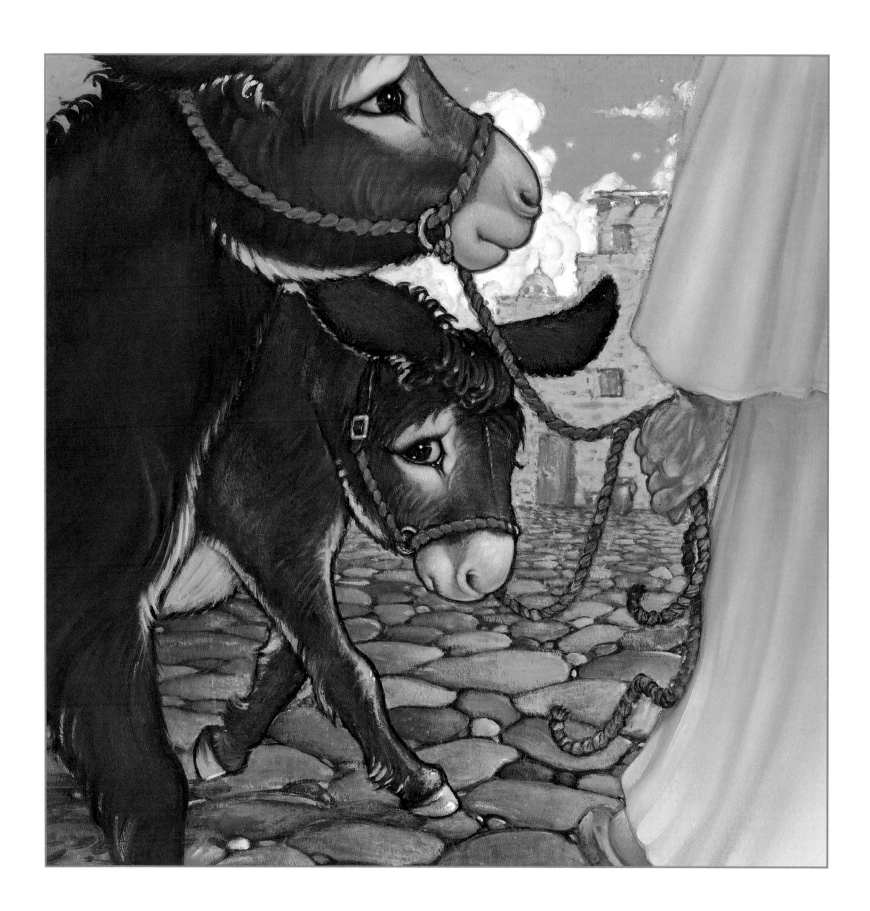

Just then, two men untied the colt.
The colt began to bray.
"Help, Mama!" cried out Little Colt.
"They're leading me away!"

But, strangely, Mama wasn't scared.
Somehow, the donkey knew
That Little Colt would be all right.
He had a job to do.

"Excuse me, sirs," the owner said.
"Don't lead my colt away."
The two men stopped and smiled and said:
"The Lord needs him today.

"We promise to return your colt,"
Assured the two nice men.
"Okay," the owner softly said.
"Do well, my little friend."

The little colt walked with the men,
Unsure of everything.
And then he met Jesus the Christ—
The King of every king!

"So, this is he," thought Little Colt.
"I feel like I should bow.
If only Mom were here with me.
Then she could teach me how."

Jesus the Christ stroked Little Colt.
He had a gentle touch.
"He's pleased with me!" thought Little Colt.
"I like him very much."

And then the men took off their coats
And pulled the colt real near.
They placed their coats upon his back,
And said, "Jesus, sit here."

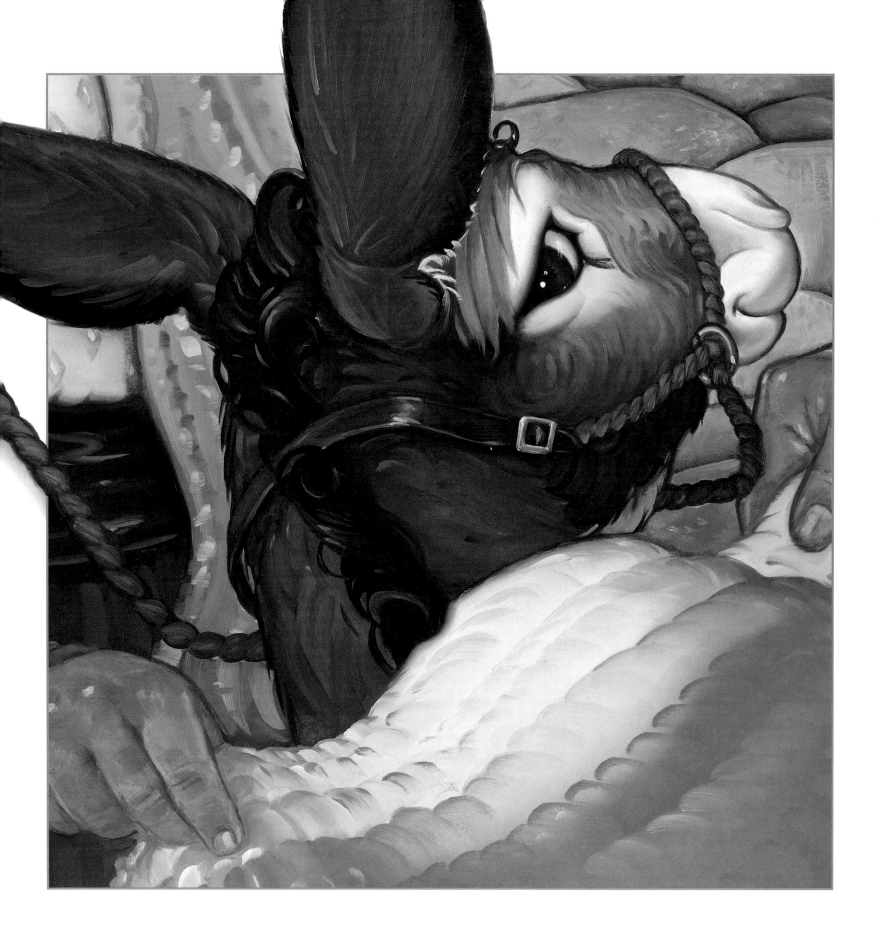

While Little Colt was glad to help,
He had a big concern:
He'd never given any rides.
He hoped that he could learn.

The Lord God climbed atop the colt.
The colt stood firm and still.
Though he was young, he understood
The need to do God's will.

Then, suddenly, a crowd appeared.

They praised the Lord and said:

"Hosanna in the highest!"

Then each man bowed his head.

The people tore off palm branches.

Some waved them in the air.

Still others placed them in the road,

And Little Colt stepped there.

The palms felt soft beneath his hooves,
Much softer than the road.
"These branches feel quite cool," thought Colt.
"And I bear a sacred load."

The crowd cheered wildly with great joy.
The colt was filled with pride.
He knew that he'd been born for this—
To give Jesus a ride.

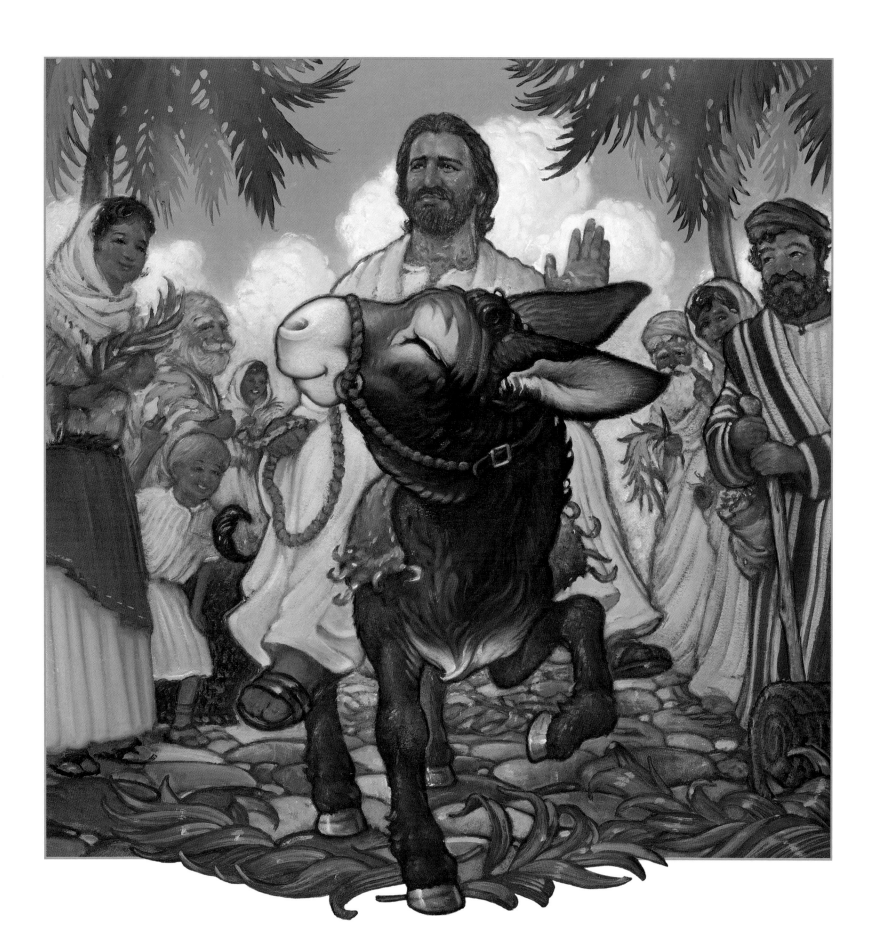

As they continued into town,
The whole world seemed to cheer.
And Mother Donkey's heart was full.
She held each moment dear.

Then Jesus climbed down off the colt.
His work had just begun.
But Little Colt had finished his;
His mission now was done.

As Little Colt watched Jesus leave,
His heart beat strong and fast.
"That ride was great!" thought Little Colt.
"If only it could last."

His insides were all fuzzy-warm.
He'd never felt this way.
He couldn't wait to tell his friends
About his special day.

He wondered if Great-Great-Grandpa
Had felt the same inside.
"Nothing compares," thought Little Colt,
"To giving God a ride."

Just then, the owner saw his colt.

"Come home now, Little One."

So, Little Colt began toward home.

His new life had begun.